HOPELESS HEROES

# HERE COMES HERCULES!

STELLA
TARAKSON

Sweet
Cherry
PUBLISHING

Published by Sweet Cherry Publishing Limited
Unit 36, Vulcan House,
Vulcan Road,
Leicester, LE5 3EF
United Kingdom

First published in the US in 2019
2019 edition

2 4 6 8 10 9 7 5 3 1

ISBN: 978-1-78226-550-4

© Stella Tarakson

Hopeless Heroes: Here Comes Hercules!

Cover design by Nick Roberts and Rhiannon Izard
Illustrations by Nick Roberts

www.sweetcherrypublishing.com

Printed and bound in India
I.TP002

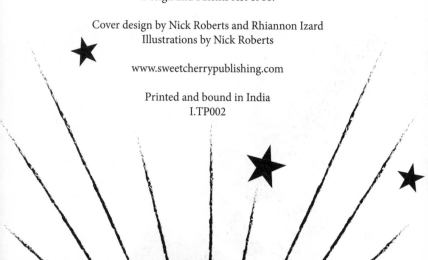

*In memory of my father, Constantine,*
*a real Greek hero*

The tiger lay at Tim Baker's feet with its mouth wide open. Its striped fur was grimy and tattered, as if it had fought in many fights. Its lips were drawn back in a snarl. Pointy yellow teeth gleamed in the fading light. They looked very sharp.

Tim felt the sweat trickle down his face. He wiped it away with the back of his hand. He had to keep going. The day was nearly over, but there was still a lot to do.

It was hot and humid and he could hear the rumble of distant thunder. The storm was getting nearer. Not looking where he was going, Tim shuffled forward. He stepped closer to the tiger, who watched and waited in silence.

Tim's foot landed inches from its head.

"Sorry," he said, edging around the massive beast. He was careful not to tread on its outstretched paws.

The tiger gazed back at him through glassy eyes. It looked like it wanted to leap up and growl. Instead it lay silent and still, poised as if ready to pounce. Tim bent down and patted its furry head. A cloud of dust flew out, which made him sneeze.

"Wow, you're dirty! Guess I'll have to clean you, too. But not now. I gotta dust before Mom comes home."

The tiger said nothing. It lay on the living room floor, watching Tim hunt reluctantly for the dustcloth.

Tim often spoke to the tiger-skin rug. It kept him company after school, while Mom was at her second job. Mom worked in an office during the day, then as a cleaner in the evening. She worked from early in the morning until dinner time. Mom didn't like being away from home for such long hours, but she had no choice. They needed the money.

Which meant Tim had to help out at home. Everyone had to pull their weight, Mom said. Tim tried. It didn't mean he had to like it.

He found the dustcloth crammed under the sofa, where he'd left it the last time he had done the dusting. Sighing, he pulled it out and turned to the mantelpiece.

First the crystal skull, then the wooden elephant. Tim's house was full of things his parents had collected from overseas. Rugs, statues, paintings … It was like living in a museum. A reminder of better

times, the jumbled collection now sat around gathering dust.

Tim moved on to the old Greek vase. It was big and black, with a narrow neck and two curved handles. Two black figures stood out on a clay-colored panel: a muscleman wrestling a fierce bull. The bull was bigger, but it looked like the man was winning.

"You know what?" Tim said to the tiger, taking a break from cleaning. "That bull looks familiar. Weird. I don't think I've met any bulls lately." He raked a hand through his mop of curly brown hair as he examined the picture closely. That wiry red hair, the stocky build, the angry face …

Tim jumped. That was it! The bull looked like Leo. Just as cross and just as stupid. If his worst enemy had horns, Leo and the bull would be twins. "I guess that's why they're called bullies," Tim muttered. "They look like bulls."

He wondered how on earth the man

could be defeating the animal. It was twice his size and pure, solid muscle. But the man looked like he was used to adventures and heroic feats. He probably wasn't stuck at home doing housework all the time. And the bull almost certainly didn't call him Cinderella!

Tim whipped the dustcloth about roughly. Everyone thought the nickname Leo had invented for him was funny. Everyone except Tim.

The vase wobbled alarmingly and started to topple. Steadying it with both hands, he gazed at the jagged writing on the vase. He wished he could read it. It might explain the man's secret. It might tell him how to defeat Leo.

"One day, I'll learn to read the words. I'll tell you what they mean," Tim told the tiger-skin rug.

The tiger looked back blankly.

"Hey, it's not easy! Even Mom can't read it. It's in Greek. The alphabet's different."

The tiger said nothing. It didn't believe him.

"I can read some of it." Tim gripped the vase carefully, the way his mother had shown him, and tilted it so he could see better. "That's an E and that looks like—"

Just then, the phone rang. Startled, Tim jerked backward, his fingers still looped around the handles.

CRASH!

The vase toppled to the floor, smashing into bits. Tim's heart beat faster. Mom would go nuts if she found out. He had to fix it, quickly, before she came home.

The phone kept ringing. Tim leaped over the pieces of broken vase to answer it.

"Hello?"

"Hi, darling." It was Mom. "Just letting you know I'm stuck in traffic. I'll be a bit late."

Tim's mind raced as he tried to remember where he'd put the superglue. "Good. I mean … okay."

Mom paused. "Is everything all right?"

"Yeah. I'm dusting, that's all."

"You're a good boy." Mom sighed. "One day, things will be different. I promise. I won't have to work long hours forever."

"I know." Tim eyed the broken pieces anxiously.

The Greek vase was the only thing in the house that was worth any money. It was very, very old – thousands of years – and that made it valuable. Sometimes Mom talked about selling it. It would bring in enough money for her to quit her second job, giving her more time at home with Tim. She could never bring herself to do it, however: the vase was the last thing Dad had given her before he died.

And now it was smashed. Scattered in

pieces across the living room floor.

And it was all Tim's fault.

"Gotta go," he chirped, trying to sound as if nothing were wrong. "See you soon!"

Tim scrambled around on his hands and knees, gathering chunks of vase. It wasn't too bad, he decided, fitting two pieces together. With a bit of luck, he could fix it so it was as good as new and Mom would never know.

"FREE AT LAST!"

a voice boomed.

Tim nearly dropped the pieces. He looked up.

And up.

And up.

An enormous man loomed above him. His legs were like tree trunks and his shoulders were as broad as the coffee table. He wore a gray garment fastened on one shoulder, exposing a muscular and hairy chest. A thick brown belt encircled his waist and his feet were thrust into the largest sandals Tim had ever seen.

"Who – who are you?" Tim's voice shook.

"Do not be afraid," the muscleman said. "I was a prisoner in the vase. You broke it and set me free." With a hand the size of a dinner plate, he helped Tim gently up to his feet.

Tim's knees had gone all wobbly. This couldn't be happening! He stared at the man in disbelief.

"How did you get in there? You're far too big."

"I was trapped by the wicked Hera." The man planted his fists on his hips and twisted his spine until it cracked. "Ah, that's better. It was cramped in there. Hot, too."

"Hang on, what did you say? The wicked who?"

"Hera. The foulest, most evil woman in the world. She is so terrible, even the rocks tremble as she passes. Don't you know her?" The muscleman's eyebrows shot up in surprise.

Tim shook his head. "Not me, sorry."

"And who are you, exactly?"

"Tim Baker."

An enthusiastic smile crept across the muscleman's face. "You're a baker?

# EXCELLENT."

He rubbed his hands together. "I'm starving. Give me two large white loaves, extra crunchy crust."

"No, I–"

"A small whole wheat loaf?"

"Baker's my name, not my job. I don't have a job. I'm ten."

The man sniffed. "You don't have a job. You haven't heard of Hera. Are you perhaps of feeble mind?"

"No kid has a job!"

"Really? I suppose I have been trapped a long time," the man admitted, stroking his wiry black beard. "Then I shall try to explain: Hera is the queen goddess, wife of my father Zeus. You've heard of the mighty Zeus, at least?"

Tim had come across that name before. Frowning, he tried to remember where. Was it in a cartoon? A book? Some sort of

story, he was sure of that.

"My father is lord of the sky and ruler of Mount Olympus," the man said, pulling himself to his full height. "You must know of him."

"Mount Olympus? Like in mythology? Greek gods and stuff?" Tim clicked his tongue. "They're just stories. They're not real."

The man lowered his bushy eyebrows as he peered down at Tim. "Not real?" he echoed, sounding displeased. "Of course they are. They're as real as me, and I am a demigod – half god, half human. Are you of poor vision? Do you doubt your own eyes?"

Tim couldn't argue with that. He said nothing.

"Queen Hera has hated me since I was born," the man continued, clenching his fists. "When I was only a few days old, she sent snakes into my crib to kill me. But I showed her: I seized the snakes and strangled them with my bare hands."

Tim felt the blood drain from his face. What sort of person would do that to a baby?

"Wh-why does she hate you?"

"She's jealous of my mother, who is far more beautiful than her. Hera never forgets an insult … and she never forgives. She trapped me in that cursed vase, snatching me from my beloved wife and daughter. Now, thanks to you, the spell is broken."

"Spell?" Tim thought for a moment. If this were really happening … if he weren't imagining things … did that mean what he thought it meant? A wide grin broke out on his face. "Hey, are you a genie? Are you going to grant me three wishes?"

"A GENIE?"

The muscleman's voice boomed across the room, rattling the windows in their frames and making Tim wince. "Do I look like a genie?"

Tim peered at the muscleman. He wasn't exactly sure what a genie was meant to look like.

"I think so," he said. "Except for the dress."

"It is not a dress! It's a chiton."

The man tugged at his short tunic.

Tim held out a piece of vase. "Genie, fix this so that it's as good as new. That's wish number one. Number two – make Leo leave me alone. And wish number three – I wish I didn't have to clean up all the time."

"Stop calling me that. I am not a genie." The man glared at him.

"Oh." That meant no wishes, Tim realized with dismay. "Then what are you?"

"I am a hero, the bravest and mightiest of them all. You must have heard of me: my name is Hercules."

Tim jumped. A real live superhero, right here in his house! That was nearly as good as a genie.

"Cool! What do you do? Can you fly?" he asked eagerly.

"No."

"Can you shoot spiderwebs out of your wrists?"

Hercules frowned and shook his head.

"Can you shoot laser beams out of your eyes?"

Hercules folded his arms across his chest and looked grumpily back at Tim.

"Well then, what *can* you do?" Tim asked. "What sort of hero are you?"

"I can do lots of things," Hercules said. "Like this." He grunted and flexed his arm muscles. They bulged like volcanoes about to erupt.

"Yes … and?"

"And this!"

Hercules lifted the sofa and raised it over his head. The wooden armrests bumped against the ceiling, leaving deep scratch marks.

"That's good," Tim said, nodding. "Can you stick this vase back together?"

Hercules let the sofa drop into place. It fell with a clatter. He peered at the pieces of vase scattered on the floor. Squatting down, he prodded them with fingers the size of sausages.

"I don't think so," he said. "The bits are too small. I can't pick them up with these super-strong fingers."

Tim sighed. "I'll fix it later." He scooped up the pieces and shoved them in a drawer, out of sight. With luck, Mom wouldn't notice that the vase was missing before he had a chance to repair it.

"Heroes don't fix pots," Hercules said scornfully. "When I was your age, I wrestled a cow with my bare hands. Have you ever wrestled a cow?"

"Um, no." Tim was trying to be polite, but didn't see how any of this would help. Flexing muscles and wrestling cattle wouldn't get the housework done.

"Cows, hmmm. That reminds me. I haven't eaten for thousands of years. Do you have any food? I'm starving."

Tim led the hero into the kitchen. Hercules sat on a cane chair. It creaked and strained under his weight. Tim opened the fridge door and peered inside. "There's some leftover roast chicken. Would you like some?"

Hercules didn't bother to answer. As soon as Tim put the platter down, the hero fell upon the chicken, slurping and chewing.

Within seconds, all that was left was bones. Burping, he wiped his mouth on the back of his hand.

Tim watched silently then cleaned up the mess. Heroes may be cool, but he couldn't help thinking a genie would be more useful.

"Thank you, Tim Baker. Heroes need food to stay strong," Hercules said, patting his stomach. "That was a good meal. How did you get the drumsticks so tender?"

But Tim was more concerned about his wishes.

"If you're not a genie, does that mean you can't help me?" he asked.

Hercules licked his fingers and looked thoughtful. "I can't fix the pot. I don't know who this Leo is and why he must leave you alone. But as for your third wish … Yes, I,

# THE MIGHTY HERCULES,

shall help you with the cleaning."

Tim brightened. Maybe heroes were useful after all! "Can you weed gardens?" he asked, thinking of all the jobs he still had to do that day.

"Weed? What is that?"

"It means you pull out the weeds – the bad plants. If you don't, they take over and kill the good plants."

"Kill, you say?" Hercules' eyebrows shot up. "Worry not. I shall save them! That's what we heroes do. Show me these evil plants at once."

Tim led Hercules out the front door.
He pointed out yellow dandelion flowers
and white clover blossoms. They nestled
among the blades of grass and peeked
out of the flower beds. "Those are weeds.
We only remove the bad plants. Nothing
else."

"It shall be done," Hercules said, locking
his fingers together and cracking his
knuckles. "Stand back, my friend. This
might be dangerous. I don't want you to
get hurt."

"It's easier to take out the weeds if you use this." Tim picked up a small spade and handed it to the hero.

Eyes shining, Hercules took it. He made slashing motions in the air.

"Dig the weeds out from the roots," Tim said, "so they don't regrow."

Hercules threw himself on the grass, flat on his stomach. He stuck his nose near a dandelion and snarled at it. "Killing the good

plants, ay? I'll soon stop you!" He lashed out
with the spade. He lopped the head off one
dandelion, then another.

# "NOT LIKE THAT!"

Tim shouted, alarmed. "That just spreads the weeds. You end up with more."

Hercules ignored him. He leaped to his feet. At super-speed, the hero darted around the garden. Ducking and bobbing, lopping the heads off all the weeds.

"How was that?" Hercules said when he came to a halt. "Are you not amazed by my strength and agility?"

Tim looked at the decapitated blossoms strewn across the garden. It would take forever to clean them up. Now he had even more work to do. He frowned.

"What's wrong?" Hercules asked, looking offended. "Are you not pleased? I did as you asked. You saw me destroy the wicked weeds."

"Ye-e-s …" Tim didn't want to hurt the hero's feelings. After all, he was only trying to help. "But that only makes them come back faster."

Hercules thrust out a huge hand, gripping Tim hard above the elbow. "You're right, my friend! I think they're growing back already. They must be like the many-headed Hydra. Every time you chopped a head off, it would grow right back."

"The what?" Tim asked, rubbing his arm.

"Hydra. A monstrous serpent with heads like giant snakes. It was so venomous, even its breath could kill. Hera created it purely so that it would destroy me."

Tim gaped. This Hera must have been truly awful.

"Do you want to know how I defeated it? I will tell you! First I covered my nose and mouth to protect myself from its foul breath." Hercules demonstrated with his free hand. "Then I cut off all of its heads as fast as I could."

With a yell, Hercules charged around the garden again, slashing and ripping with the spade. This time, he sliced up all the flowers too. Roses, daisies, petunias.

"No, no!" Tim ran behind him, waving his arms and shouting. Hercules didn't listen. He kept on slicing until there were no flowers left.

Panting, Hercules came to a standstill. He gazed proudly across the lawn. "Then I made my brilliant discovery. There is only one sure way to stop the Hydra heads from returning. Fire! Burn the neck stumps and the heads can't grow back."

The hero reached into his tunic and pulled out a small, gray rock. He scraped it with a sharp fingernail until a small flame emerged.

"No!" Tim yelped, guessing what was about to happen.

# "STOP!"

"Don't worry, I'll stop the Hydra weeds," Hercules said, setting a dry branch alight. He lifted the flaming torch to the sky. "Because I'm a hero!"

Before Tim could stop him, Hercules took off. Racing around the garden, the hero seared all the plant stems with the burning torch. He burned weeds and flowers alike. Soon all that was left was a blackened, smoking mess. Small flames erupted here and there and Tim chased after them, kicking up clods of dirt to put them out.

Hercules extinguished the torch with a flourish.

"There! I have saved your garden. No, don't thank me. That's what heroes are for."

"Saved it? You've ruined it! How am I ever going to explain …?" The words died in Tim's throat as Mom's car pulled up.

Still wearing her cleaner's uniform, Mom climbed out of the car. She looked tired. Her shoulders were slumped and she was walking slowly. When she saw the smoldering garden, however, she rushed to the gate. Her eyes bulged.

"Tim! Are you all right?" She gripped him by the shoulders. "What on earth happened?"

"You know the difference between make-believe and the truth, don't you?" Mom asked.

Tim and Mom were sitting at the kitchen table. It was time for dinner. Tim was very hungry but Mom wanted to talk.

"Yes. I'm telling you the truth."

"I'm not angry." Mom was using her patient voice. She reached out and held Tim's hand. "Why did you burn the garden? Tell me what's upsetting you."

"Nothing. I keep telling you. I didn't burn anything."

Mom tried again. "I know you don't like cleaning. And I know you get lonely after school."

"It's not that," Tim said, his freckled nose twitching with emotion. He had told Mom everything. Everything ... except for the bit about breaking the vase. It was still in the drawer, where it would stay hidden until Tim found a chance to fix it.

He'd explained that an Ancient Greek hero had suddenly appeared in the living room and offered to help with the housework. The hero didn't know much about weeding and was only doing what he thought was right. Mom didn't believe Tim. She thought he had made Hercules up.

"But, but, he's here. Can't you see? In that chair." Tim pointed.

Mom looked through Hercules as if he weren't there. "That's enough." She was starting to sound cross. "Imagination is good but you're taking it too far, Timothy."

Mom only called him that when she was angry.

Tim looked helplessly across the table.

"You can see me," the hero said, "because you set me free. No one else can see or hear me."

"This is terrible," Tim said. What was the point of an invisible hero? Who would believe him?

"Don't worry." Mom thought Tim was talking to her. "I know what the problem is. You're lonely. You're upset because I'm away all day."

"That's not–"

Mom patted his cheek distractedly and kept talking. "One day I'll get promoted at my office job. One day a publisher will like my stories and make them into books. And, eventually, we'll have enough money for me to quit my second job. Then I'll be able to spend more time at home with you."

Hercules sniffed. He wiped a tear from his eye. "That's so sad. I know how your mother feels. I miss my family too: I wish I could be at home with them. I hope your mother succeeds in her honorable quest."

"Mom'll make it," Tim whispered. "She writes great stories."

Mom leaned over and gave Tim a quick hug.

"Thank you for believing in me. It helps." Sighing, she stood and trudged over to the fridge. "It's time to eat. I'm glad we've got leftover chicken. I'm too tired to cook."

"Ah …"

Mom spun around, her long ponytail flying. "Where is it? Did you eat it? How did you eat it all? It was almost a

# WHOLE CHICKEN!"

"Hercules ate it. Heroes get hungry."

Mom stared at Tim. He could tell she was trying not to lose her temper. Her cheeks turned red and her back stiffened. "I guess you won't want any dinner, not after eating all of that."

"But I'm starving! I haven't eaten anything. Honest."

"I don't feel like cooking. We'll have salad."

Tim's shoulders drooped. He hated salad.

Hercules burped and smiled. It was the sort of smile people have when they're full of roast chicken. Tim's stomach growled unhappily as Mom sliced tomatoes and cucumbers and piled them high on their plates.

■　■　■

The next morning, Mom drank her coffee and ran out the front door.

"Bye, dear. See you tonight!" She was in a hurry as usual.

Loud snoring drifted out from the living room. Tim stuck his head through the doorway. Hercules was fast asleep on the sofa, mouth open, long leg dangling over the armrest. Tim tiptoed past. He didn't want to wake him. Heroes needed their sleep.

Tim decided to do some cleaning now, early in the day, so there'd be less to do later.

"Where should I start?" Then he remembered. The tiger-skin rug. It was very dusty.

The rug was heavier than he'd expected. Tim gripped the tiger's ears with both hands and then heaved. He dragged it down the hall and out the back door. Getting it onto the clothes line took all of his strength. He pulled and tugged and hauled. Finally, the stuffed head flopped over the line. The tiger snarled silently and its eyes bulged.

"Don't worry, this won't hurt a bit," Tim said. "Soon have you good as new." He fastened some clothespins on the tiger's fur to stop it from sliding off. He shook it. A cloud of dust flew out, making him sneeze. He needed something to hit the rug with. "Hang on. I'll get my cricket bat."

The tiger didn't reply. It hung patiently on the clothes line, staring across the lawn, and down toward the creek that bubbled and tumbled noisily through the bottom of the garden. Tim ran into the shed and fetched his bat. When he returned, Hercules was standing at the back door, stretching and yawning.

"Good morning," Tim said. "How'd you sleep?"

Hercules ran his hands through his hair. "Not very well. Your sofa is too …"

Tim didn't find out what was wrong with the sofa, however, because Hercules suddenly gave a loud yell.

# "BEWARE! A TIGER!

A vicious, man-eating tiger. Right behind you!"

"No, it's just—"

Pausing only to flex his muscles, the hero rushed to Tim's side. "Do not fear, Tim Baker, the mighty Hercules will save you!"

"You don't need to save me," Tim said, prodding the tiger-skin rug with the cricket bat. "It's not dangerous: it's just a rug."

"Don't you believe it. Once a man-eater, always a man-eater. And you, my friend, are snack-sized."

Hercules pulled the bat out of Tim's hands. He poked at the stuffed head. The rug swayed back and forth on the clothes line. "See how it threatens us? It prepares to pounce."

"But it's dead."

"That's what it wants you to think." Hercules growled at the tiger. "You can't fool me, vile beast."

Tim took his bat back and put it down a safe distance away. "It's just a–" he started to say.

"Hah!"

Tim looked on, horrified, as Hercules dragged the tiger skin to the ground. The hero and the rug rolled around and around the backyard. One moment Hercules was on top, the next moment the rug was. Soil and bits of grass clung to the tiger skin. It was dirtier than ever.

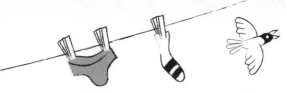

As they tussled, Hercules glared at the tiger's jaws. "I've beaten mightier foes than you. Even the Lion of Nemea, the most fearsome beast in the world."

The tiger didn't answer. It flopped bonelessly as Hercules kept on rolling and talking.

"That ugly cat was a man-eater. Its hide was so thick, no weapon could pierce it. I was the only one strong enough to defeat it. Do you want to know how I did it?"

The tiger's head nodded limply.

"Don't try making friends with me," Hercules hissed. "You don't fool me that easily." With one powerful leap, Hercules flipped them both over so that the skin was pinned beneath his knees.

"I didn't need a weapon," Hercules continued, scowling into the tiger's face. "I killed it with my bare hands, then I cut through its skin with its own sharp claws. And guess what? I turned that tough lion into a cloak. I'd give up now if I were you."

Suddenly, there was a loud ripping sound. A long tear appeared in the tiger-skin rug, all the way from its tail to its front paw.

"That's more like it." Jumping to his feet, Hercules slapped the dirt off his hands. "Victory is mine!"

Tim groaned. How was he going to fix the rug without Mom finding out? After the fiasco with the garden, she'd be sure to think that Tim had been deliberately destructive.

Hercules picked up the torn skin and examined it. He looked at Tim with a pitying expression. "I hate to say this, my

friend, but you were wrong. This is not a man-eater after all! It's just a skin. See?" Hercules slung the rug on like a cloak. The tiger's jaw rested on his forehead like a hat.

Tim opened his mouth to explain then changed his mind. There was no point. Hercules might be super-strong, but he wasn't super-smart.

"For you." Hercules took the skin off and wrapped it gently around Tim.

It was hot and heavy and itchy. Tim felt his knees sag from the weight.

"Wear this cloak to school," Hercules said. "It shall protect you from arrows."

"I don't *need* to be protected from arrows."

"Of course you do. Skinny little lad like you. You need all the help you can get."

"Get it off me! It's heavy."

Hercules plucked the rug off Tim as easily as if it were a dishcloth. He carried it back into the living room and spread it out on the floor.

"Fine," said the hero. "But you know where it is if you ever need it."

Tim ran into the bathroom and returned with a soft towel. He used it to cover up the tear in the rug.

"I'll fix you later," he whispered into the tiger's ear. "Good as new. I promise."

Straightening, Tim turned to Hercules. "I have to go to school now."

"I shall come with you. To keep you safe."

"You don't need to," Tim said, backing away. He didn't think he could cope with any more protection. "School's not far. I always walk by myself."

Hercules squatted down so he could look Tim in the eye. "You don't need to be alone anymore. You've got me now."

Tim thought the hero looked sad. "Um, thanks, but …" he started to say.

"Being your hero makes me feel better. I miss my little girl. I haven't always been a good father," he mumbled, his dark eyes haunted. "That evil Hera tormented me and never gave me peace. She drove me insane. But then I met my new wife and we had Zoe, and I vowed to keep them safe forever." A giant tear trickled down the hero's cheek.

"I – I'm sorry." Tim tried to hide his surprise. He didn't know that heroes cried.

Hercules sniffed. "All I want is to go home and protect my wife and daughter. I can't, I know. But now I've got you to look after." He smiled at Tim. "And I'm going to do the job properly," he added, wiping away the tear.

"Okay." Tim didn't know what else to say. "Thanks."

Looking happier, Hercules followed Tim out the front door. The garden was blackened and Tim tried not to look at it.

"Are you sure no one else can see you?" he asked worriedly. What would his teacher say? Taking heroes to school was probably against the rules.

"Sure I'm sure. Look." Hercules waved at a mother with a stroller. She looked right through him and kept on walking.

Tim nodded, relieved. As they turned a corner, Hercules suddenly stiffened. Tim followed his gaze. An old lady was walking a dog. The dog was big and black and strong. It bristled at the sight of them. Looking straight at Hercules, it showed its teeth and growled.

"It can see you," Tim whispered, alarmed. "Quick, let's cross the road."

Hercules' eyes narrowed. He locked his fingers together and cracked his knuckles. "No need to be frightened, Tim Baker. You've got me to protect you now!

# STAND BACK!

I don't want you to get hurt."

# 7

"I – I don't need to be protected," Tim stammered. "It's much easier to just cross the road." He looked at the big dog in alarm. It continued to stare and growl at them.

Hercules stared and growled back. "You know, that mutt looks familiar ..." His voice trailed off as he squinted hard at the dog.

"How come it can see you when nobody else can?" Tim kept his voice to a low whisper so that the old lady wouldn't hear him. He didn't want her to think he was talking to himself.

"Dogs have superpowers too. Their noses can smell the sweat on a flea," Hercules said. "And if it's what I think … if I remember rightly … this beast is more powerful than most."

"B-beast?" Tim didn't like the sound of that. He put a restraining hand on Hercules' arm. "It's not a–"

"Cerberus!" Hercules roared. "We meet again!"

The dog barked an angry reply.

"Who …?"

"Cerberus, you hellhound! I shall banish you back to the Underworld, where you belong. What have you done with your other two heads?"

"His what?"

"He has three heads, all with razor-sharp fangs. One bite and you're done for."

"This dog's only got one head." Tim felt he should point that out.

"It likes to hide the other two. Don't be fooled. King Eurystheus gave me twelve labors to prove my strength. Capturing Cerberus was the final test, which I passed brilliantly of course. I'd know that beast anywhere." Hercules' gaze never wavered from the dog.

"That was a long time ago." Sweat broke out on Tim's brow. "It can't be the same dog."

# "CERBERUS, YOU FIEND!

Lying in wait to exact your revenge. You shall not have it."

"It's not a fiend – it's a pet," Tim said, gripping Hercules more tightly. "Look, it's got an owner."

Hercules peered at the old lady holding the leash. She was glancing around nervously, clearly wondering what was upsetting her dog. Tim glanced away and tried to act casual, as if it had nothing to do with him.

"Calm down, boy," she murmured. She looked scared.

"See how Cerberus frightens her? I shall save her. Fear not, old woman, Hercules is here!" He shook off Tim's hand and strode purposefully toward the dog.

Frenzied barking filled the air. Lunging forward, the dog pulled free of its owner's grasp. It threw itself at Hercules, growling and snapping.

"Think you're stronger than me?" the hero snarled. "I'll teach you!" With one hand, he picked the dog up and

raised it high in the air. The dog paddled its feet wildly and snapped its jaws.

# "ADMIT DEFEAT, VILE HOUND!"

The old lady's hand fluttered to her mouth. Tim realized how preposterous this would appear to her. She couldn't see Hercules, so it must look as though her dog were floating.

"Put. It. Down." Tim ordered.

Hercules lowered the dog to the ground. He briskly wrapped the leash around its paws. The dog struggled and whimpered, but it couldn't move. Making soothing noises, the old lady bustled over to her pet. She started to unwind the leash, darting nervous glances at Tim. She must have noticed that her pet had stopped levitating as soon as Tim spoke. The dog licked her hand and wagged its tail. Tim was glad it was all right.

"Let's go," he said, tugging at Hercules' chiton. He had to get them away from there. "I can't be late for school."

"Oh. Right." Hercules looked at the lady patting the dog. "The beast has been subdued and the old woman is safe now. All thanks to me." He puffed out his chest proudly.

■　■　■

Luckily school was only a few streets away. As they approached the gate, Tim turned to Hercules and said, "This is it:

we're here. You can go home now."

"I shall stay and protect you."

"No, that's okay. I'm fine."

But Hercules stood his ground and folded his arms as if the matter were settled.

Tim couldn't risk it. Who knew what trouble Hercules would cause at school?

"I don't need protecting!" Tim thought quickly. "I need help. I need you to go home and sweep. Do you know how to sweep?" He mimed a broom-swishing action.

"Of course I do," Hercules scoffed. "I'm the mightiest sweeper in the world. In fact, I can super-sweep. Wait and see." He spun on his feet and hurried away.

Tim's shoulders sagged with relief. Turning, he trudged across the playground.

"Who were you talking to?" It was his best friend, Ajay, falling into step beside him.

Tim jumped. He hadn't noticed him approaching.

## "WHAT? WHEN? NO ONE."

"At the gate. It looked like you were talking, but there wasn't anyone there. Were you talking to yourself?" Ajay barked with laughter, his soft black eyes sparkling.

"Yes. Yes, I was." Tim nodded vigorously.

Ajay flashed him a suspicious glance. "What's going on? Tell me."

Tim was tempted. What was the point of having an exciting secret if he couldn't share it with his best friend? He hesitated for a moment and then the words tumbled out in a rush. "All right. But only if you promise not to tell anyone."

"I promise."

Tim dropped his voice as they approached their classroom. "I've got a hero."

"Big deal," Ajay said, dumping his bag on the floor outside the room. "Lots of people have heroes. Mine's Harry Potter."

"No, I mean a real one, not a story one. He's in my house."

"Huh? Whaddya mean?"

In a low voice, Tim told Ajay everything.

Ajay's eyes grew wider and wider and brighter and brighter. When Tim finally stopped talking, Ajay punched him softly on the arm.

"You're joking."

"It's true," Tim insisted. "Hercules said he'd help me with the cleaning but–"

"What's up, Cinderella?" A sneering voice cut off his sentence. Tim whirled around to see Leo sneering at him. His worst enemy was standing right behind them! Tim wondered how much he'd heard.

Too much, as it turned out.

"You need a fairy godmother, not a hero!" Leo brayed. "Dude, you can't even lie properly."

"Go away," Ajay snapped. "No one's talking to you."

Leo snickered as he plucked a jelly bean out of his pocket and popped it into his mouth. "Hey, do you want me to punch Tim too?" he said to Ajay. Leo clenched his hand into a fist and thrust it near Tim's face. "I can punch harder. Here, I'll show you." He drew back his meaty arm.

Tim flinched and closed his eyes. He expected to feel searing pain as his nose was mashed against his face. Instead, he heard footsteps, the clacking sound of high heels tapping impatiently across the asphalt toward them.

"What are you boys doing here?" It was their teacher's voice. "The bell's about to ring. Time to line up for assembly. Off you go." Miss Omiros shooed them away with a flick of her long red fingernails.

"Lucky for you this time, loser," Leo said, dropping his fist and sticking his face near Tim's. He came so close that Tim could smell his sickly sweet breath.

"Next time, you're gonna need your hero to save you. Pity he's not real."

The school day passed in misery. Leo teased Tim about Hercules every chance he could. Ajay stood up for Tim, but it was clear he didn't believe him either. By the end of the day Tim was sick of it. He wished he'd kept Hercules a secret.

"Aren't you going to show me your hero?" Leo asked when the last bell rang.

Tim gritted his teeth. "I can't. He's invisible."

"Right. Invisible, oh yeah I forgot. Still, I wanna see your burned garden. And the ripped tiger rug." Leo curled his hands into fists and cracked his knuckles. "Then I might believe you."

"I'm busy," Tim said, turning away.

"Will you be okay?" Ajay asked, taking a halting step toward him. "I'll walk home with you if you like."

"Nah, I'll be all right."

Tim was glad Ajay wanted to help, but couldn't help feeling a little annoyed that his best friend hadn't believed his big secret. In any case, if Leo wanted to get mean, there wasn't much Ajay could do to stop him. Leo was bigger than both of them. It was far better to avoid a confrontation, and get home as quickly as possible.

Tim decided not to mention his other worry. He remembered the hero boasting about being able to super-sweep. Tim wondered what that meant. He had a sinking feeling he was about to find out. Without looking back, Tim hurried out of the school gate and down the road. His pulse quickened when he heard Leo lumbering after him.

"HEY! CINDERELLA!

Slow down. What's the rush? Bet ya can't wait to show me your secret hero." Leo snickered unpleasantly.

Tim ignored him. Picking up his pace, he sprinted as fast as his legs would carry him, his backpack thumping against his back. He should be able to outpace the bully. Leo was big, but he was heavy. He lurched rather than walked. Soon Tim was pushing open his front gate. He hurried to the front door.

The door opened and Hercules stepped out. "Welcome home, my friend! Come in and see–"

"Hey, dude! For real? You actually burned your garden?" Leo panted as he approached the house. The bully was faster than he looked. "Didn't your mom tell you not to play with matches?"

"Who is this fat worm?" Hercules asked, his eyes narrowing.

"Don't worry about him. Let's go inside."

Tim tried to dart around Hercules but the hero held him back.

"What does he want?"

"Trouble," Tim said, pressing his lips together.

"Then he shall have it!" Hercules boomed, his face like thunder.

"Let's just go inside."

Leo smirked. "Talking to yourself now?

Man oh man. You're even crazier than I
thought."

"Allow me to chain that worm to a rock,"
Hercules said. "I shall set eagles to peck out
his liver and rats to feast on his eyeballs."

Tim shuddered. "Please, no. Just, um,
show me your super-sweeping."

Hercules' eyes brightened. "You want
to see? Right. Follow me."

But first he took a deep
breath and turned toward Leo.
Puffing out his cheeks, the hero blew a
long stream of air straight at the bully.
It made the leaves rustle in the trees and
the dirt skitter along the ground. Leo
staggered backward as if he had been
pushed by an invisible hand. He tripped
and fell hard, his teeth snapping together.
His face clouded with fury.

"Ouch! You pushed me! How'd ya do
that?"

Tim didn't answer him. He tugged on Hercules' arm. "Let's go."

"If you insist," Hercules said, still glaring at up Leo, "but I was enjoying myself."

Tim slammed the front door and locked it. Feeling better, he walked down the hallway. It was good to have a hero. Leo would think twice about coming back!

Tim started to relax, until he entered the living room. It was completely empty. No sofa, no television, no coffee table. The usually overloaded mantelpiece was bare. With a sinking feeling in the pit of his stomach, Tim darted up the stairs and into the first bedroom – Mom's room. The bed, chest and wardrobe had all vanished. Not a stick of furniture remained. Gasping, he dashed to his own bedroom. It was utterly bare too.

Tim rushed from room to room, eyes bulging. "Where's all our stuff gone?"

"HAH! I WILL SHOW YOU."

Tim followed Hercules into the backyard. Spread across the garden were the contents of the entire house. From fence to fence, right down to the creek at the bottom of the garden. Beds, tables, chairs. Books, shoes, cups. All piled high in messy heaps.

"I super-swept. The house has never been cleaner!"

Tim's hands shook. He didn't think he could take much more today.

"You're supposed to sweep out the dirt, not the whole house! Quick, we've got to put everything back before Mom comes home. She'll go nuts!"

"If you insist." Hercules looked displeased. "But I think I did a good job."

Tim and his hero raced around. Huffing and puffing, they put things back as fast as they could, racing to finish before Mom returned.

They almost made it.

▪ ▪ ▪

Mom arrived while Tim was picking the final fork out of the flower bed. Shading her eyes, she stood at the back door and called out. "What on earth are you doing?"

Tim ran over to her, dirt sprinkling

onto the ground.

"Ah. Err. Hi. You see, Hercules tried to help with the cleaning …"

"*Don't* start that again. I'm not in the mood for stories." Mom rubbed her eyes and stomped off into the kitchen.

Something had upset her, Tim could tell. Something more serious than grubby cutlery.

Sighing, Mom threw herself into a chair. "My book's been rejected again. That's the tenth time. Guess I should give up now."

Tim was stunned. Mom never talked about giving up. "You can't. You said you'd always keep trying. That one day you'd make it."

"I've been fooling myself. It's not fair on you, darling. All these dreams of being a writer, they're a waste of time."

"They're not."

Mom cupped his chin and smiled. It was a sad smile. "I have to get real. I'm not going to get published. There's only one way I can make enough money to quit my second job. We'll have to sell the old Greek vase."

There was a pause. It was long and uncomfortable. It felt like time had slowed down. Tim could hear the clock ticking out the seconds in the hallway.

"Mom. There's something I have to tell you. That vase." Tim gulped. "I broke it."

Mom shook her head, as if she hadn't heard properly. "What was that, dear?"

"I broke the vase. I'm so sorry. I was cleaning it; the phone rang and …"

Mom's face went white with shock. She didn't look angry. Just sad.

"I was going to glue it back together," Tim added, "and make it good as new."

"Let me see. We might be able to fix it." Mom heaved herself out of the chair and followed Tim into the living room.

With shaking hands, Tim pulled the pieces out of the drawer and spread them out in a neat row near the tiger-skin rug. Together they sat on the floor and looked at the broken vase. It was like a giant jigsaw puzzle. Mom's shoulders drooped as she tried to fit a few of the pieces together.

"That's Hercules, fighting a bull. It was one of his twelve labors." She smiled sadly at the picture. "Your father bought this for me because he said I was bullheaded."

Tim gave her a puzzled look. "Your head doesn't look like a bull's."

Mom chuckled. "I'm glad to hear it."

Tim peered at the drawing. The bull

didn't look anything like Mom. Then again, the muscleman didn't look much like Hercules either.

Mom picked up more chunks of vase and looked at the Greek letters despondently. "I've always wondered what this says. Now I'll never know."

"Does that mean we can't put it back together?" Tim asked, his fingernails digging into his palms.

"We can, but there's no point. The vase will be worthless. No one will pay good money for something that's been repaired in so many places. Pity." She sighed.

Tim buried his face in Mom's shoulder. "Now you'll have to keep working forever. It's all my fault."

"Hey, that's okay. Don't cry."

"I'm not crying," Tim said, blinking rapidly. "I got dust in my eye. I haven't cleaned up in here yet."

Mom engulfed Tim in a huge hug. Tears glistened in her eyes. "Bad things

happen for a reason," she murmured into his mop of hair. "Guess this means I have to keep writing. The next story will be better. Someone will like it. You'll see."

∎　∎　∎

Although he didn't get in trouble for breaking the vase, Tim went to bed feeling terrible. He'd glued the vase together, just in case … but Mom was right. It was covered with so many criss-crossing fracture lines that it looked like a spiderweb was wrapped around it.

Nobody would pay for a vase like that.

The next morning Tim awoke to silence. Something was wrong. It took him a moment to realize what it was: Hercules was not snoring.

Tim leaped out of bed, ran down the stairs and into the living room. Hercules wasn't asleep on the sofa. Tim hoped the hero hadn't decided to do some early morning cleaning. Suddenly, a loud thud came from the kitchen. Fearful of what he might find, Tim inched down the hallway. Another thud. Followed by a burp.

"Very tasty," Hercules said as Tim walked in. "What else have you got?" The floor was littered with empty food packets. Cereal, biscuits, cakes. All opened, eaten, and dumped onto the floor.

"Not much, by the look of it," Tim replied, sizing up the pantry.

"What's this?" Hercules held up a can of peaches. "The picture on it shows fruit,

but when I tried to bite it, it tasted of metal."

"The fruit's inside," Tim explained. "You need a can opener. I'll get it."

But he didn't need to bother. Before Tim had a chance to move, Hercules squeezed out the can's contents as if it were a tube of toothpaste.

"Lovely," he slurped. "Is there any more?"

"Later. Help me clean this mess before Mom sees it."

Tim opened the garbage can to throw out the empty food packets. He froze.

Mom's story was there, covered in crumbs. She had given up! Tim pulled the pages out and spread them neatly on the kitchen table. They weren't rubbish. Maybe if Mom saw that Tim had saved them, she'd start working on the story again.

"You'd better stay at school with me today," Tim said as they cleaned up. He couldn't risk leaving Hercules home alone again. "But you have to behave. Can you do that?"

"Me? Of course I can. Why, I'll super-behave! You'll see."

Tim kept his fingers crossed all the way to school. Part of him was worried that Hercules might cause trouble. Another part was glad to have the hero with him, in case Leo wanted revenge for being knocked to the ground.

"Sit in the playground and wait for me," Tim told Hercules as they walked through the gate. He pointed to a long metal bench outside his classroom door. "Don't move from here."

"Hey! Talking to invisible heroes again? Man oh man, you need help." Leo seemed to appear out of nowhere. He looked around uncertainly, then bumped Tim hard with his bag, sending him sprawling on his hands and knees. "That's for knocking me over yesterday," he hissed. "I don't know how you did it, but …" Still glancing left and right, Leo turned and strode away.

Hercules helped Tim to his feet. He dusted him off.

"Are you hurt? I shall swat that worm like the insect he is," the hero growled.

"I'd rather forget it."

"Why do you let him treat you like that?" Hercules asked, bending down and peering into Tim's face.

Tim shrugged miserably. His knees stung and bits of gravel clung to his palms.

"Tim Baker, you have to stand up for yourself."

"How?"

# "WRESTLE HIM.

Throw him to the floor and tie him up with stout ropes. That's what I did with the wild pig of Erymanthus. It should work: that boy looks like a pig."

"I – I don't think that's a good idea." Tim adjusted his collar, which had twisted sideways as he fell. "He's bigger than me."

The hero snorted. "It matters not. I have defeated monsters taller than trees, mightier than mountains. It's easy. I shall show you how."

Just then, the morning bell rang. All the children started to dash toward the assembly area. "Don't do anything!" Tim begged. "I've got to line up with the others. Just sit on the bench and don't move. Please."

"All right, I will wait," Hercules agreed. "But remember what I said. Say the word, and the bully shall be beaten."

Hercules strode toward the bench and sat down. His legs were so long that his knees pressed up against his chest. The bench sagged under his weight, bending at the middle.

All morning, Tim darted glances through the open classroom door. Sure enough, Hercules stayed on the seat. He twiddled his thumbs. He chewed his nails. But he did not move. Tim started to relax. Maybe everything would be all right. Leo was ignoring him and Hercules was behaving.

Two hours passed and it was nearly time for recess.

That was when the trouble began.

From the corner of his eye, Tim saw
something move. He snapped his head
around. Hercules had left the bench. He
had come up to the classroom. Right
outside, where all the backpacks were lined
up.

"Food, I need food," Hercules mumbled.

"Psst," Tim hissed from the corner of
his mouth. "Go away!"

Either Hercules couldn't hear, or he

ignored Tim's warning. The hero plunged his hand into someone's bag. Grinning, he pulled out an apple. It was gone in one gulp. Hercules stuck his hand in another bag, then another. Each time he found more food and swallowed it whole.

"No!" Tim shouted, forgetting to be quiet.

"Is there a problem?" Miss Omiros asked, her heels tapping across the floor.

Tim opened and closed his mouth. Just as he was trying to work out what to say, the bell rang for recess.

"I'll talk to you later, Tim," the teacher said. "You may all get your morning snacks and go outside."

Chattering happily, the children ran over to their backpacks.

"What was that about?" Ajay asked as he rummaged for his recess snack. "Hercules causing trouble again?"

"Yes," Tim said, even though he knew that Ajay was only teasing.

Tim watched as one by one the children went to Miss Omiros to complain that someone had taken their food.

"I bet it was Tim," Leo told her, his lip curling. "He's so poor, he has to steal to eat."

"That's enough, Leo," Miss Omiros said sharply. "Go outside."

Tim turned to go too, but the teacher stopped him.

"Tim, I want to see your backpack."

"You can't believe Leo!" Ajay piped up. "He's just being mean."

"I know. But I noticed Tim was the only one not to look in his backpack. Why not?"

Tim couldn't tell the teacher the real reason. Hercules had eaten all of his food on the way to school, so he knew there'd be nothing to eat.

"I – I …" Tim shifted his weight from

one foot to the other.

"Who were you talking to before?"

"Nobody. I was – uh – thinking out loud." Tim looked across the playground warily. After gobbling everyone's lunches, Hercules had disappeared. Tim had to find him before he managed to eat all the food in the school.

"Show me your backpack. I want to look inside."

Tim hurriedly opened his backpack for Miss Omiros.

There was no food in it.

"All right," the teacher said, eyes narrowing. "You may go play. But I'll be watching you."

Tim didn't have time to worry about

that. He had to find Hercules. Heart pounding, he ran across the playground. He thought he knew where Hercules would be.

In the cafeteria.

He was right. Behind the counter, next to the lunch ladies, was his hero. Unseen by everyone except Tim, Hercules picked his way through a jar of breadsticks. Munching and crunching and chomping.

Barging to the front of the line, Tim shouted, "No, don't eat that!"

Everyone turned and stared. Tim knew he looked crazy, but he had no choice. He had to get Hercules out of there.

"Go to the end of the line," one of the lunch ladies said, glaring at him. She was standing right next to the ancient hero.

"Put down that muffin!" Tim ordered, glaring at Hercules. "And go home."

The plump woman sucked in her breath. "Who do you think you're talking to, young man?"

"I can't say," Tim said. Then he added to

Hercules, "You've had more than enough already. You'll get fat."

"How dare you?" the woman said shrilly, holding in her stomach.

Hercules licked his lips as he picked up a sandwich. "All right, my friend. I'll go as soon as I finish this."

Tim's head drooped. He felt relieved. But not for long.

A hand fell on his shoulder. It was Miss Omiros. "Tim Baker. You're coming to see the principal. Right now."

■   ■   ■

"Not fair," Tim mumbled on his way home. Lunchtime detention. He hadn't called the cafeteria lady fat! He'd been talking to Hercules.

After much thought, Tim had decided to tell the principal the truth. An invisible hero was on the loose. Tim had been trying to stop him. The principal had pressed her lips together in a long, thin line. She didn't believe Tim. No one ever did. From now on, he would keep Hercules a dead secret … from everybody.

Faint with hunger from a day without food, Tim entered the kitchen, hoping he could find something to eat. What he saw made him wish he had after-school detention, too.

Flour was strewn all over the floor. Cracked eggs were splattered on the tiles. Mixing bowls and frying pans sat in rivers

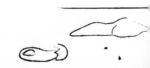

of butter. Tim leaped over a milk puddle.

"What happened?" he yelped.

"Pancakes," Hercules replied, brushing crumbs off his chiton. "I was feeling hungry. Do you like pancakes? I used to make them for my daughter."

"How will I ever clean it?" Tim felt like tearing out his hair.

"Worry not, I've fixed bigger messes than this. One of my labors was to clean the Augean Stables. You wouldn't believe how dirty they were. The smell! Piles of horse dung this high." Hercules held his hand up to his forehead. "And I only had one day to do it."

"Did you manage?" Tim's voice shook.

"Of course I did. Sit down. I shall show you how."

Tim paced nervously as Hercules marched out through the back door. He was doubtful, but what choice did he have? There was no way he could clean all that mess by himself. Soon a scraping, digging sound came from outside. It started at the back door, and moved gradually farther away. Right down to the creek that flowed through the bottom of the garden.

Suddenly, the digging was replaced by a

gurgling sound. Like running water.

With a loud *WHOOSH!* a torrent
of creek water sped into the kitchen. It
covered the floor. It soaked Tim's ankles.
It lapped against the cabinet doors. Within
seconds the water was waist-deep. It
churned through the room, swirling the
flour and eggs into a sticky underwater
cyclone.

"This is how I cleaned the stables!"
Hercules shouted over the noise.

"Aargh! A flood, a flood!"

"Pretty smart, eh?"

Tim didn't answer. The water was
creeping up his chest. Wet leaves from

the creek clung to his shirt and pants. He scrambled up onto the kitchen table and gaped at the swilling waters below. Tim was a strong swimmer, but hoped it wouldn't come to that.

"Don't worry, my friend. It's under control."

Hercules thrust his big hands into the water and pushed. The water bubbled and

seethed. Then it rushed outside. Hercules forced it all the way back to the creek. The floor was sopping wet … but sparkling clean. All traces of dirt and debris had been washed away.

Dripping, Tim jumped to the floor. He rushed to the back door and watched the creek water recede to its proper place.

"See?" Hercules said, wiping his hands on a dry bit of chiton. "All done. Nothing to worry about."

Except for one thing. Tim's face turned white when he saw it.

Mom's story had been swept off the kitchen table by the flood waters! Washed up in a corner, the pages were soaked right through. Shrieking, Tim tried to scoop it up. It was so soggy it fell apart in his hands.

# HER STORY WAS RUINED!

Tim attempted to wring the water out but that just made the problem worse.

He was still trying to stick the torn pages together when Mom came home. They were damp and the sticky tape kept peeling off.

"What happened?" Mom asked, splashing across the kitchen tiles. "How did you get so wet? Why's there water on the floor?"

"Your story." Tim's voice trembled as he held up the sodden pages. "It's wrecked. I'm sorry."

"Never mind about that. It's only a copy. The manuscript's still on the computer." Mom waved the paper away as she opened a cabinet and looked under the sink. "Maybe a water pipe burst. Hmm. Doesn't look like it. Strange."

Tim didn't know what to say. Hercules sat in a kitchen chair and watched with a smile on his face.

Mom looked at Tim, eyebrows lowered. "Timothy. *Where* did all this water come from? I want the truth."

The truth? Last time he'd told the truth, he'd got detention. Besides, Mom would say he was making things up again. He turned away.

"You won't believe me."

Mom groaned. She splashed over to
Tim and put an arm around his shoulders.
"I'll try," she said. "You can always talk to
me. I won't get angry. Promise."

Tim looked up at his mom. She looked
back. Tim took a deep breath, as if he
were about to dive into a swimming pool.

He would take a chance. He would try sharing his secret, one last time.

"I think you should sit down."

He told Mom everything. Right from the beginning. He told her about Hercules being trapped in the vase, and how he escaped when it broke. Tim told her about the weeding. About the tiger-skin rug. About the pancakes and the creek water.

Mom didn't interrupt. She sat quietly with her hands folded in her lap. Her eyes grew bigger and brighter. When Tim finished, he looked at her nervously. Did she believe him?

"Brilliant," she said. "What a great idea!"

Beaming, she jumped to her feet. She grabbed a notebook and pen, scribbled and muttered, "He thought the dog was Cerberus!" She chuckled. "Right. I've got to write this now, before I forget it." Mom bustled off to her bedroom, where she kept her computer. She looked excited, the way she always did when she started a new story.

A huge weight lifted from Tim's shoulders. Mom hadn't laughed at him. She hadn't got angry. He wasn't too sure she believed him, but she looked happy. Tim didn't feel so bad about breaking the vase now.

Which reminded him … he'd been meaning to show Hercules something. This was as good a time as any.

"Hey, Hercules. Come and look at this."

Tim squelched his way into the living room, trying not to drip onto the tiger-skin rug. He grabbed the glued-together vase and flashed it at the hero. "See this muscleman? It's meant to be you."

Hercules peered over Tim's shoulder and grunted. "Me? Humph! In real life, I am much stronger." He flexed his muscles to demonstrate. "At least it shows I'm winning the fight. I beat that bullheaded bull easily."

"Is that what this says? How you beat the bully?" Tim turned the vase carefully, showing Hercules the lines of writing on the back.

The hero let out a loud gasp. "Can – can you give it to me?"

"Sure. Why?"

"The writing. I can read it! It says …
it says …" Hercules fell silent. His lips
moved as he read the ancient words.
It took a long time. He clenched and
unclenched his fists.

Finally Hercules looked up, his face
white with shock.

"My friend. You will never believe what
it says."

"Tell me. What does it say?" Tim asked, staring at the writing on the vase.

The hero's lips trembled. "It says there's a way to send me home. Back to my wife and daughter. Thank the gods; I've missed them so much!"

Tim couldn't help grinning. "How? How do we do it?"

"We have to do what the vase says. I haven't got to that bit yet … but I, Hercules, shall do whatever it takes. Do I need to wrestle a bull? Easy! Do I need to hold up the sky? Simple!"

"Well, what does it say?" Tim asked, wishing he could read it himself; it would be quicker.

Hercules peered at the jagged writing, his brow furrowing with the effort. It took a long time, but Tim kept quiet. When Hercules finally finished, his eyelids drooped and his shoulders slumped. He looked at Tim, his face a mask of misery.

"What's wrong?" Tim asked. Surely his hero could do anything!

"It is too hard. I thought it might be hero work, but it's not. It's … a puzzle."

Startled, Tim jumped. He loved puzzles.

"You probably haven't noticed, but I'm not very smart. Surprising I know. But now I'll never go home." Hercules started to cry. Big fat tears trickled down his cheeks. They splashed onto the floor.

"I'm good at puzzles," Tim said hastily. He had to stop Hercules from crying before the house was flooded again.

"You are?" A look of hope flashed across the hero's face. "Can you help me go home, Tim Baker?"

Tim didn't want Hercules to go. Despite the trouble he'd caused, Tim liked him. Besides, it was kind of cool to know a hero, even if he did have to keep it a secret from most people. But Hercules looked so sad, and he missed his family so much …

"I'm sure I can," Tim replied firmly. "What sort of puzzle is it?"

Hercules sniffed. "I have to solve a riddle. A riddle! How ridiculous!

Why can't it say hold back the ocean, something simple like that?"

"Read it out."

"Hang on, I have to find it again." Hercules ran a finger down the vase. "Here we go. It says:

> *If you have me, you want to share me.*
> *If you share me, I won't exist.*
> *What am I?"*

Mouth hanging open, Tim stared at Hercules.

"What's the answer?" Hercules asked eagerly. "Speak it, so I may go home."

"I'm sorry," Tim had to say. "I've no idea."

"Guess," Hercules urged. "You said you were good at puzzles."

Gazing into the distance, Tim rubbed his chin. "Hmm. What do you want to share, but if you do, it stops existing?"

"That's easy," Hercules said, holding his stomach. "I'm not so dumb after all. Food! If you share food, it no longer exists. Because it gets eaten."

Tim frowned. He wasn't too sure.

"Go on, try that. You have to be the one to say the answer," Hercules explained, "because you freed me."

Tim shrugged. It was worth a try. "Okay. Food."

They waited. Nothing happened. Hercules was still there.

"It's wrong, it's wrong," the hero groaned.

"What do I want to share?" Tim asked

himself. "Toys? Games? No, they'll exist even if I share them. Hmm."

"How about housework?" Hercules suggested. "When you share it, it gets done faster."

"That might work! Let's try: housework." Again, nothing happened. Hercules kicked a chair glumly. It snapped in half.

"Don't worry," Tim said, eyeing the broken chair. "We'll work it out. It just takes time. Hey, is that the answer? Time?" He waited a few seconds. "Oh. Guess not."

"This won't work. I'll never go home." Hercules stamped his foot impatiently. The floor shook and the windows rattled.

"Wait, there might be a clue on the vase. What else does it say?"

The hero's eyes shifted left and right.

"Nothing."

"But – but it must say more," Tim protested. "Look at all those sentences! You've only read a few lines."

"They … say nothing." Hercules didn't sound very convincing.

Tim wondered what the hero was trying to hide – and why. "Well, who wrote the riddle?" he asked. "Does it say that, at least?"

"Yes." Hercules lowered himself to the floor as if exhausted. He mopped his brow. "These are the words of my father, the mighty Zeus, King of the Olympians."

Tim nodded, waiting for more.

"My father wants me to be able to go home – but only if I can prove myself worthy. Zeus was never happy with my report cards. He used to chain me to a cliff face until I had finished my homework. But hah!" For a moment Hercules looked his old self again.

"No chains could hold me! I snapped them like fish bones and escaped." Then his eyes drooped again. "Maybe that was a mistake."

"That's okay." Tim leaned down and patted the hero awkwardly on the shoulder. "We'll work it out together."

Tim tried different answers all evening. None of them worked. No matter how many times he tried, he couldn't guess the answer to the riddle.

The next morning, Hercules was lying on the sofa with his hands over his face.

"Any ideas?" he asked as Tim entered the room.

"Not yet, but I'm still trying. Do you want some breakfast?"

Hercules sighed. "No thanks. I'm not hungry."

Tim's eyebrows shot up. "Not hungry? You?" Tim was worried. Hercules was always hungry. "Are you coming to school with me today?"

"I'll stay here if you don't mind. I won't clean. I won't cook. I just want to sit."

Tim didn't want to leave Hercules alone when he looked so sad. He had no choice, though. He had to go to school.

"Don't worry. I'll keep working on the puzzle," Tim promised. "I know I can do it." And he crossed his fingers for luck.

Tim headed toward the front door, then paused. He was sure there was more written on the vase than Hercules was letting on. What if it could help him solve the riddle? Tim didn't know whether the hero had trouble reading – or whether it said something he didn't want Tim to know.

But maybe there was a way to find out. Miss Omiros. His teacher was Greek –

she'd mentioned it in class one day.

Tim tiptoed back into the living room. He didn't want Hercules to see what he was about to do and ask awkward questions. He needn't have worried. Hercules was lying on the sofa with his hand over his eyes. Loud snoring filled the room. The hero had gone back to sleep.

Grabbing the vase by its handles, Tim hefted it off the mantelpiece. He left the house as quietly as he could. Once outside, Tim slung his backpack on his back and cradled the vase in his arms. It was big and slippery. Tim had to be very careful; it wouldn't survive another fall. If the vase broke, Hercules might be stranded forever, even if they did manage to solve the riddle. No magic vase, no magic. It stood to reason.

"What're you doing with that?" Ajay asked as Tim trudged across the playground. He hurried over to help. They took a handle each and carried it between them.

"Thanks." Tim rolled his aching shoulders with relief. "I'm taking it to Miss Omiros. See if she can read it."

"How come?"

They were interrupted before Tim could answer.

# "HEY! CINDERELLA!

What's that ya got?" Leo strode toward them, popping jelly beans into his mouth as he walked.

"None of your business," Tim snapped, not slowing his pace. "C'mon Ajay, ignore him."

"It's not show-and-tell today. Whaddya bring that ugly thing for?"

Tim pressed his lips together and kept walking. He didn't look back. With his free hand, he knocked on the teachers' lounge door. Miss Omiros opened it, a mug of coffee in her hand.

"Miss," Tim panted, hoisting the vase up higher. "Can I show you something?"

The teacher let out a low whistle. "Oh my, an amphora." She put her mug down before plucking the vase delicately from Tim and Ajay's hands. "The Ancient Greeks used them to store wine and oil, did you know that?"

Tim shrugged. He knew for a fact they also used them to store heroes, but decided not to mention that.

"Do you know how old it is?" the teacher asked.

"Dunno exactly. Very old. It broke, though, and I had to glue it back together. Can you read what it says?" Tim showed her the writing on the back. "Mom said it's Greek."

Frowning, Miss Omiros ran her long red nails over the letters. Tim held his breath. What would it say? Finally, after what felt like ages, the teacher shook her head. "No, I'm sorry. It's in Ancient Greek. I only know modern. Some of the words are familiar, but not enough. I've no idea, sorry."

"Do you know anyone who might?" Tim dared to hope, but Miss Omiros shook her head.

Tim's heart sank. His plan had failed. He was no further forward. The riddle was still unsolved.

He left the vase in the teachers' lounge for safekeeping, then went to class. He hoped Hercules wouldn't notice the vase was missing and come to school to investigate. There was no sign of the hero all day, however. In a way that was worse. Tim hoped Hercules wasn't feeling too upset.

■ ■ ■

After the last bell rang, Tim went to the teachers' lounge to collect the vase. He went alone. Ajay had cricket practice straight after school and couldn't help. Tim gripped the vase with both arms and headed for home. It seemed to grow heavier with each step. Sweat dripped off his face and he had to stop to rest several times. It was like carrying a large, fat baby in his arms; a grouchy, slippery baby that kept trying to slide from his grip.

"Nearly there. I can do it," Tim muttered as he turned the corner onto his street.

Then he froze.

Waiting in front of his house, swinging on the gate, was Leo. The rusty hinges creaked in protest, setting a neighbor's dog barking. Tim had thought Leo wouldn't dare turn up again, not after being flattened by Hercules last time. What did the bully want?

"Shouldn't you be at home?" Tim asked, trying to play it cool. "Your parents'll be worried."

To Tim's surprise, Leo's face flushed

bright red.

"Don't talk about my parents!" He kicked the gate with a scuffed shoe. "Just shut your face."

"All right," Tim said. He had no idea what *that* was about. He tried to edge past the bully. "Whatever. I've got to go in now."

"Not until you show me what you've got," Leo said, his voice fierce.

Tim tightened his grip. "It's just an old vase. Nothing special."

"Yeah? Then give it to me." Leo jerked forward and snatched the vase out of Tim's arms.

"Hey, give it back!"

"Not until you tell me what you did

before. You knocked me down without touching me. How'd ya do it?"

"I didn't." Tim lunged for the vase but missed. "It … it was the wind."

"Tell me or I'm gonna drop it." Leo lifted the vase up high, too high for Tim to reach.

"All right." Tim's mouth felt dry. He had to say something. He couldn't let Leo destroy Hercules' only chance to go home. "I didn't do anything. It … it was my hero."

Leo rolled his eyes. "Not that hero stuff again. Prove it! Go on. If he's real, I want to see him."

Leo tossed the vase into the air. Tim's breath jammed in his throat. He didn't exhale again until Leo caught it. "Put it down, please."

"Call your hero, Cinderella, or I'll drop it."

Tim had no choice. He darted past Leo and unlocked the front door.

# "HERCULES!"

he shouted down the hallway. "Hercules, come quickly! I need help."

Tim and Leo stood breathing heavily, eyes fixed on the doorway. Watching. Waiting.

Nothing happened.

Hercules did not come.

14

"Pah, I knew it!" Leo spat when Hercules didn't appear. "You're such a liar. There's no hero. You made it up to sound cool."

"No I didn't—" Tim stopped when Leo drew his arms back, his grip on the vase loosening.

"I'm gonna smash it. There's no such thing as heroes, Cinderella."

Tim's mind raced. He had to think of something. For some reason, Hercules wasn't answering his call. It was up to Tim to stop Leo. Like the bull on the vase, the bully was too big to wrestle, but …

Tim's thoughts flew back to the very first time he had met Hercules. He remembered how surprised he'd been to learn that Hera had sent snakes to kill the infant demigod. It gave him an idea.

"Then watch out for the snake!" Tim cried, throwing up his hands.

Leo's arms paused in mid-air. "What snake?" A note of uncertainty entered his voice.

"In the vase," Tim said, struggling to keep his face straight. "I keep my snake in there. I took it to school to show Miss, to see if I can bring it for pet day."

"There's no snake." Leo lowered the vase, holding it as far from his chest as possible. His hands shook slightly.

"Yeah there is. His name is Hercules. After the Ancient Greek hero."

Leo crinkled his nose. "Is that what all this hero stuff's been about? A stupid snake?"

"Yes." Tim nodded, letting Leo believe the lie. "Why, did you think I meant a real hero?" Tim snorted and shook his head.

"But I heard you tell Ajay—"

Tim didn't let Leo finish his sentence. "Miss said I can't bring the snake for pet day because it's too dangerous. That's why they had to keep it in the teachers' lounge."

"Too dangerous?" Leo's hands shook harder.

"It's an adder, very venomous. I didn't know that when I trapped it. But I'm not worried. Hercules likes me." Tim paused and glanced pointedly at the vase. "I don't think he'll like you, though."

"You're making it up," Leo said, his face rigid with fear.

"Oh yeah? Stick your hand in and see."

"You're weird, ya know that? You can keep your stupid snake." Leo put the vase carefully on the ground and backed away.

"Come near me again, and I'll set my hero on you!" Tim lunged toward Leo.

# "GARR!"

Leo turned and fled.

"See if I care. You're still a loser. I'll get you later!" he shouted as he ran, his cheeks wobbling with the effort.

Tim wiped the sweat off his brow and took a deep breath. It had been a close call, but he'd made it.

When his heart went back to normal, he picked up the vase and carried it inside.

. . .

Hercules was still lying on the sofa, his eyes closed. Tim eased the vase back onto the mantelpiece. He cleared his throat.

"No luck, then," Hercules said, opening one eye. "You could not solve the cursed riddle. I can tell, because I'm still here."

Tim shook his head. Thanks to Leo, he'd almost forgotten about the riddle. "You?"

"No. Guess we shall have to give up." He sighed gustily.

"Don't say that, we'll–" Tim stopped. Someone had opened the front door and was walking down the hallway. It was way too early for Mom to come home from work. Had something bad happened?

"Hi, darling." Mom breezed into the living room. A big smile lit up her face. "Guess what? I'm not going to my second job today. I've taken the day off!"

"Did she get fired?" Hercules moaned. "This is a bad day for everyone."

Tim flapped his hand at him to be quiet. He knew it wasn't that. Mom looked too happy.

"I've been to see a publisher. They loved the idea for my new story. They want to publish it!"

"YAY!"

Tim threw himself into her arms. In that instant, he forgot all about Leo. Mom might be able to leave her second job!

"Does that mean you'll always come home early?"

"Eventually. Maybe. It'll take a while, mind you, but one day it might happen. Then you won't have to do all the housework anymore."

Tim grinned. That was good, but having Mom home was better.

"All thanks to you." Mom gave Tim a loud kiss on the cheek. Her lipstick left a sticky patch. Tim wriggled uncomfortably. "My story's called *Hercules the Housekeeper*," Mom continued, licking her thumb and wiping off the red mark from Tim's face. "He's strong but makes mistakes. He gets into all sorts of trouble. You gave me the idea when you shared your wonderful secret with me."

Hercules groaned from the sofa, but Tim didn't turn his head to look. He stared at his mom. "Does that mean you believed me? You know I didn't make him up?"

Mom didn't answer. Instead she said, "How about we get takeout to celebrate? Today's too special for grilled cheese sandwiches."

"Yeah! Can we have chicken and fries?" Tim picked something he knew Hercules would like. He wanted to share his happiness with his friend. Maybe the food would help cheer him up.

"You bet," Mom said, patting Tim's cheek. "I'll go get it. Want to come with me?"

Suddenly Tim froze. Something

Mom said had given him a clue. Finally, everything clicked into place. He knew the answer to the puzzle!

"Um, no. That's okay. I'll stay here."

"Sure? All right. Won't be long."

Tim waited impatiently for Mom to go. As soon as he heard the front door click shut, he darted to the sofa and whispered in Hercules' ear.

Delighted, the hero leaped to his feet.

"Yes, that sounds right. It must be it." Hercules engulfed Tim in a giant hug. Tim felt his ribs creak under the pressure. "I don't know how to thank you, Tim Baker."

"You don't need to thank me," Tim gasped, pulling away and rubbing at his sides. "You helped me too. I couldn't get all three wishes but I got one …"

Hercules looked puzzled; then his face broke into a giant grin. "You beat the bully?"

"Yep. I did." Tim nodded.

"Did you do what I told you?

Did you tie him up with ropes? Chain him to a boulder? Pick him up and hurl him into the deepest pits of the Underworld?"

"Nope, nothing like that." Tim's eyes glowed. "Something better: I tricked him."

Hercules raised his eyebrows. "With your brain? You are clever indeed. Puzzle solver and bully beater!" He reached over and ruffled Tim's hair, making it stand up in wild tufts. "And now, thanks to you, I can see my wife and daughter again. Agatha, Zoe, I am coming home!" Tears filled Hercules' eyes.

Tim didn't want his hero to leave, but he knew he had to let him go. "Are you ready?" Tim whispered, smoothing his hair back down. "Shall we do it now?"

"Yes. Now." Hercules pulled himself to

his full height. "I'll say the riddle and you answer it. Here we go:

*If you have me, you want to share me.*
*If you share me, I won't exist.*
*What am I?"*

Tim smiled. He nodded once, twice. Then he spoke.

"A secret."

Sparkles of golden light shone around the hero. "It's working. I can feel it. Goodbye, Tim Baker. I will always remember you, my clever friend!"

Hercules waved as the sparkles grew bigger and brighter, forming a thick shimmering mist.

Then it vanished, along with the hero. Tim was alone in the room.

But not for long.

Mom would be back soon with a celebration feast.

That night, Tim awoke to an unfamiliar noise. Something was moving about in the darkness. Groggy with sleep, he opened his eyes. Tim always slept with his bedroom door open. The house was pitch black: the only light was the soft gray square of his bedroom window.

His first thought was that Hercules must be hunting for a midnight snack. It was the wrong sort of sound, however.

This was stealthy. Sneaky. A soft scraping, a few seconds of silence, then a slither. Hercules wouldn't be so quiet. Hercules would stomp around the kitchen noisily, not creep along the hallway like an oversized snake.

Then Tim remembered. The hero had gone home. It couldn't be him.

Maybe it was Mom moving about. But wouldn't she turn on the light?

Tim climbed out of bed.

As quietly as he could, he stepped out onto the landing. The sound was coming from downstairs. He darted into Mom's room. He could see her dark outline in bed.

"Mom," he whispered, tugging at the blankets. "Wake up."

"Mmmm … wha …" Mom mumbled.

"There's someone in the house."

"Thass nice … say hi …" she rolled over to face the wall.

"Mom," Tim spoke more urgently. The sound of her soft snoring filled the room.

Another bump, then a crash. Tim jumped. He wished Hercules was still there. Heart pounding, Tim shut his mother's door. He inched down the staircase. He could hear voices coming from the living room. A woman's and a man's.

# INTRUDERS!

They spoke softly. Tim had to creep closer to hear what they were saying.

"I can't see it anywhere, Your Majesty."

"It's here. I know it is," the woman hissed. "Look harder!"

"Yes, Your Majesty." A bump, followed by a curse. "I'm trying, but it's too dark."

The woman let out an irritated sigh. Then Tim heard the sound of fingers clicking. The room flooded with dazzling light. Keeping to the shadows, he peered through the doorway. It took his eyes a moment to adjust. He rubbed them, wondering if he was seeing things.

Standing in the middle of the room were two shimmering figures. A tall, thin woman with jet-black hair and very pale skin. She wore a long, ivory-colored gown. On her head was a dainty crown with a transparent veil trailing down the back. Next to her was a young man in a short white chiton. His cap and sandals had feathery wings attached to them. They fluttered as he stumbled around the room.

"Find it. Find it now," the woman commanded.

"Yes, Your Majesty." The young man bumped into a potted plant, knocking it sideways. It screeched as it skidded across the floorboards.

"Careful, you clumsy oaf! Do you wish to awaken the household?"

"Yes, Your Majesty. I mean no, Your Majesty." The young man ducked and bowed. "Forgive me, Queen Hera."

Tim jumped as he recognized the name. This was the evil woman who had trapped Hercules in the vase! What was she doing here?

"Find what I seek. Retrieve my vase at once, Hermes, or your punishment shall be severe."

She wanted the vase back! Tim's breath caught in his throat.

"It's hard to find anything in this mess," the man called Hermes complained, nudging a cushion aside with his foot.

"No excuses!" Hera hissed. "This *is* the home of Tim Baker, is it not?"

"It is, Your Majesty." As if gathering courage, Hermes shook himself before continuing. "Maybe he read the writing on the vase, my Queen. Maybe he figured out what it can do."

"Nonsense," Hera snapped. "He would not have sufficient wit."

"Hercules said the boy is smart."

Hera snorted. "That idiot! A slug is smart compared to Hercules." Hera's pale blue eyes were like chips of ice. "Now the buffoon walks around town as if he owns the place. I won't have it! I shall trap him again, this time forever. But first – find my vase."

"Didn't Hercules say it was broken? They might have thrown it out."

"They did not! It is here. I can feel its presence. They must have repaired it." Hera swayed like a snake as she strode around the room. "Where is it? Where?!"

"Maybe in here, Your Majesty," Hermes said, peering inside the fireplace.

Not looking where he was going, he stumbled over the tiger-skin rug. "Yah!"

Arms spinning wildly, he jerked backward, knocking the queen goddess over. She sprawled on the ground in an undignified heap, her crown pushed sideways.

"YOU IDIOT!"

Hera cursed, straightening her veil. "Can't you see where you're going? No – do not touch me." She ignored the trembling hand Hermes extended. She rose to her feet in one fluid motion. "Look at what you've done." Hera held out her index finger and shook it menacingly.

Tim squinted, trying to see what she was talking about.

"You chipped my nail, Hermes. Now I'll have to go home and file it."

Hermes shrank backward. "I'm so sorry, Your Majesty. Forgive me."

"You fool. Take me home, then return at once. Find the vase. Do not dare to show your face until you succeed." Hera held out her hand regally. Hermes, bowing, took her hand and they shot up to the ceiling before vanishing. Tim gaped, stunned. Seconds later, Hermes reappeared, this time on his own.

The young man stumbled around the room, wings flapping frantically as he searched. Tim eyed the vase on the mantelpiece. He had to stop Hermes from taking it. But how?

"Ah." Hermes spotted the vase. His eyes glittered.

"Garr!" With an ear-piercing shout, Tim flung himself into the room. He swept past Hermes, who spun around in bewilderment. Moving quickly, Tim lunged for the vase. He clasped it in his arms and held on tight.

"Give it to me, boy." Hermes' voice was sharp.

"NO."

"You must."

Tim pressed his lips into a thin, hard line.

"If you don't, Hera will punish you. She'll come back and snare you." Head drooping, Hermes added in a softer voice, "She'll punish me, too."

Tim lifted the vase high into the air. "Come closer and I'll smash it," he warned, silently thanking Leo for giving him the idea. The last thing Tim wanted was to break the vase. He wanted to keep it as a reminder of

his hero, but the bluff might just work.

Hermes' chin wobbled. "I'll tell the queen on you. She'll be very angry. You won't get away with this, Tim Baker." The wings on his cap and sandals flapped more vigorously. The young man floated up to the ceiling, where he bobbed up and down. "You'll see!" And then he vanished.

Shaking, Tim cradled the vase and took it into his bedroom. From now on, he would have to keep a very close eye on it. For Hercules' sake …

… and for his own.

Look out for Tim's next ADVENTURE!

# HOPELESS HEROES

# HERA'S TERRIBLE TRAP!

Sweet Cherry Publishing

STELLA TARAKSON

# 1

Tim Baker wrapped his scarf around his neck. It was unusually cold for May. The clouds were heavy with rain despite the fine weather forecast. As if defying the television weatherperson, a splatter of rain plonked firmly onto Tim's forehead and slithered down his nose.

He shuddered.

There were plenty of other things he'd rather be doing on a soggy Sunday

morning. Like playing computer games
in his cozy living room. Or chatting with
his best friend, Ajay. Or even – yep – *even*
finishing off his math homework. But no.
He couldn't do any of those things. Tim
fished a damp tissue out of his pocket and
blew his nose glumly.

An outdoor garden center! Of all things! Row after row of nothing but leaves, stems and petals. And a whole bunch of adults in raincoats nodding and making *ooh* and *ah* sounds, as if they'd never seen a plant before. Really, didn't they have anything better to do with their time?

Not that there was anything amazing waiting for him at home, Tim realized, a lump forming in his throat. Not since his good friend Hercules had left.

Tim's adventures had started when he accidentally broke an Ancient Greek vase his mother owned. Incredibly, an enormous figure had erupted out through the cracks. At first Tim thought he'd released a genie. Instead it turned out to be the hero Hercules. Half human, half god, Hercules was the son of a mortal woman and Zeus, king of the Olympian gods. Not what you normally find in a vase, but since then Tim had learned to expect the unexpected.

Hercules had been trapped in the vase thousands of years ago by Hera, Zeus' wife. The queen goddess was jealous of Hercules' beautiful mother. From the moment the demigod was born, Hera had decided to hate and resent him. If it hadn't been for Tim's accident, the hero would still be in the vase now, perched on the mantelpiece—a terrible secret trapped forever.

"Come along, dear, keep up," Tim's mother said as she strode past some hyacinths.

"Can we go home now?" Tim asked, picking up his pace.

"Not yet."

"But it's cold." He glanced at the sky. "And it's starting to rain."

Mom muttered something under her breath and kept walking.

Tim tried again. "I'm bored."

Mom turned and fixed Tim with a penetrating stare. "We wouldn't be here at all, if it weren't for ... well, you know why." She pressed her lips together and put a tray of petunias in her cart.

Mom didn't say it out loud but Tim

knew what she meant. If he hadn't destroyed their garden, she wouldn't need to replant it. Except … he hadn't been the one to slash and burn all their flowers. It had been Hercules.

Asking the hero for help with the weeding had turned out to be a big mistake. How was Tim to know that Hercules thought plants had to be fought off like the Hydra, a multi-headed monster whose heads grew back after being sliced off? Hercules was super-strong but not exactly super-smart. Even so, he'd proved to be a loyal friend. He had sided with him against Leo the bully, and encouraged Tim to stand up for himself. Despite all the trouble he'd caused at home and at school,

Tim missed Hercules. There had been no such thing as boredom when the hero was around.

Unlike now.

Sighing, Tim trailed after his mother as she turned yet another corner.

And fell flat on his face.

■　■　■

Malicious laughter erupted above him. Tim looked up to see his worst enemy, Leo, looming over him, a grin on his flushed face.

# "OOPS! CLUMSY."

Leo snickered.

Tim knew very well that he'd been tripped on purpose. He pulled himself to his feet with as much dignity as he could muster.

"What are you doing here, Cinderella?"

Leo used the nickname that he'd made up. It was a cruel dig at the fact that Tim did housework. Not that he wanted to, of course, but Mom worked two jobs and he had to help out. That didn't stop the bully from teasing him about it, however.

"Having fun looking at the flowers, are you? Find anything nice?" Leo pursed his lips in a mock pout and fluttered his eyelashes.

Was it worth pointing out that Leo was at the garden center too? Tim paused, pondering the best way to put this.

The bully must have misinterpreted

Tim's thoughtful expression for one of fear.

"Go on, go find your mommy," Leo sneered. "Maybe she'll buy you a pretty flower so you won't cry."

Normally Tim would walk away, preferring to avoid trouble rather than tackle it head-on. But since he'd outsmarted Leo once before, he'd grown bolder in their encounters.

"Yeah, I'm just chilling." Tim folded his arms and ignored the dirt and dead leaves clinging to his pants. "But why are *you* here? Have you suddenly become a botanist?"

Leo narrowed his eyes and didn't answer. Tim suspected the bully was

trying to work out what a botanist was,
and whether he'd just been insulted.
Shrugging, Leo pulled a bag of jelly beans
out of his pocket and popped a red one
into his mouth.

Tim's stomach growled at the sight of the food. He hadn't eaten since breakfast and it was nearly lunchtime. He clamped a hand over his gut, hoping Leo hadn't heard.

"Ooh, would ya like one?" Leo patted the bulging bag. "Sorry, I'm all out."

"Leo! Where've you got to? Leo!"

The angry voice grew louder. Tim saw a small woman striding toward them, her head darting from side to side like a bird of prey. Her gray hair was pulled back in a severe bun and her eyes flashed behind thick glasses.

"Here, Grandma," Leo called out half-heartedly. He dropped his gaze to the ground.

"Where? Drat the boy. Always wandering off. One of these days I'll …"

"I said here!" Leo turned toward the small figure, a look of misery on his face. "You're lucky I'm busy," he shot over his shoulder at Tim. "Otherwise I'd slug you."

Tim hesitated – but only for a moment. Just as Leo started to walk away, Tim put his foot out.

"Oops! Clumsy." Tim repeated Leo's excuse as the bully fell face first into the dirt.

Leo grunted as he hit the ground, hard.
Tim darted off before the bully had
a chance to pull himself upright, the
words "I'll get you for that, Cinderella!"
ringing in his ears.

Tim realized that giving Leo a taste
of his own medicine probably wasn't the
smartest thing to do, but he knew that
Hercules would have been proud. Acting
quickly, Tim thrust himself into a group

of chattering old ladies clustered around
a stand of waving sunflowers. Leo would
think twice about following him into
their midst, especially with his grandma

watching. Concerned about drawing
attention to himself, Tim tried to look
interested in the display.

It was the first time he'd ever seen a
sunflower up close. Something caught his
eye. Its bright yellow
head was filled
with pointy
little seeds.
Tim had eaten
sunflower
seeds many
times before
as a snack, but
had never been
bored enough to
give them much

thought. But now – safe from Leo and with Mom still shopping – he had plenty of time to kill. He peered at the blossom. How exactly did the seeds come out? Did they fall when you shook them? Experimenting, Tim grasped the flower's long stalk and shook it gingerly.

Nothing happened.

He tried a bit harder.

Still nothing.

And a little bit harder …

"Hey! Whaddya think you're doing?"

The voice of a store assistant took Tim by surprise. Startled, he jerked back, snapping the stem clean through.

"YOU CAN'T DO THAT!

The assistant started wading through the crowd of shoppers in Tim's direction, an angry look on his face.

With the sunflower still in his hand, Tim ran the opposite way. Any minute now the assistant might call the police

– and then he'd really be in trouble. They wouldn't believe it was an accident. They'd think he was a vandal. Or a thief. Quick, he had to hide the evidence! Panting, Tim scrunched the flower up in his palm and shoved it in his pants pocket.

"Tim! There you are. Slow down!" Mom wheeled her laden cart over to him and put her hand on his shoulder. "Where did you vanish to?"

"Mom. Can we go now? Please." He tried not to sound frantic.

Mom looked Tim up and down, taking in his wild expression and heaving chest.

"What's up?"

"Nothing. I–"

"Madam, your son has been damaging

❧◇❧

store property." The assistant caught up with them, huffing and puffing, his face redder than the store's roses. He was carrying the pot with the decapitated sunflower.

"Why? What did he do?" Mom gripped Tim's shoulder harder than was necessary.

"This." The assistant hoisted up the plant. "I'm afraid you'll have to buy it."

Mom looked like she was about to argue, but then changed her mind. "Yes, all right. I'm sorry about that. I'm sure it was an accident."

The assistant sniffed in disbelief and plunked the severed plant into Mom's cart. He glared at Tim, then flounced away.

"Would you care to explain that,

Timothy?" Mom asked as they got in line for the register. She only called him Timothy when she was angry.

"It was an accident! I was just looking at it. I didn't mean to break it."

"What is it with you and flowers?"

Tim didn't know what to say.

"At least you didn't set fire to anything," she said wryly. Tim couldn't tell whether she was joking or not. "Come on, help me unload the cart. When we get home I'll make us some lunch. Spaghetti okay?"

Tim's gurgling stomach answered for him.

■　■　■

Mom bustled around the kitchen, cooking and humming a cheerful tune.

She'd been in a good mood ever since a publisher had accepted her book – which was probably why Tim wasn't in trouble for breaking the sunflower. Thankfully she'd believed him when he'd said it was an accident. Mom had been busier than ever lately, but she was happy and that made her nicer. Most of the time.

Tugging off his rain-spattered coat, Tim ran into his bedroom to check on the vase. Hercules ought to be happy too, he thought, now that he finally had what he wanted. By solving a tricky riddle printed on the vase, Tim had been able to send the demigod back to his family in Ancient Greece. For the third time that day, Tim made sure that the vase was still in his wardrobe. He whipped off the sheet that cloaked it and there it was, its fracture lines visible even in the gloomy light.

A few days ago Tim had removed the glued-together vase from the living room mantelpiece and put it where he could keep a close eye on it. Mom didn't seem to mind.

Although he didn't say why, Tim had a very good reason for wanting to keep the vase hidden. Not long after Hercules had left, two intruders had entered Tim's house in the dead of night. They tried to steal the vase from right under Tim's horrified gaze. One was the evil goddess Hera, who wanted to use the vase to recapture Hercules. The other intruder was her servant, a young man called

Hermes. He had wings on his cap and sandals and used them to fly. Hermes was clearly terrified of Hera, which only reinforced all of the awful things Hercules had said about her.

Tim had managed to stop them from taking the vase, but the flying guy had threatened to return. Tim kept his gaze on the big black vessel as he started to unknot his scarf. Hermes and Hera could come back at any–

"Hey!" Tim yelped, his eyes bulging.

The vase! It was floating!

At first it looked like there was nobody holding it, but Hermes gradually materialized. His body shimmered as it solidified in front of Tim's eyes. The intruder's gaze sharpened when he saw Tim watching him.

"Got it!" Hermes crowed. "Sweet. Hera will be delighted." The wings on his cap and sandals started to flap vigorously and he rose into the air. "So long, pal!"

"No-o-o-o!" Without thinking, Tim rushed at the flying figure. He jumped,